This book belongs to

The Heine Family

Mr. Bliss.

Mr. Bliss

J.R.R.TOLKIEN

Boston
HOUGHTON MIFFLIN COMPANY
1983

First American Edition 1983

Library of Congress Cataloging in Publication Data

Tolkien, J.R.R. (John Ronald Reuel), 1892–1973.
  Mr. Bliss.

  "The manuscript of Mr. Bliss is owned by Marquette University, Milwaukee, Wisconsin" – T.p. verso.
  Summary: Mr. Bliss's first outing in his new motorcar, shared with several friends, bears, dogs, and a donkey, though not the Girabbit, proves to be unconventional though not inexpensive.
  [1. Humorous stories] I. Title. II. Title: Mister Bliss.
PZ7.T5744Mr 1983   [Fic]   82-15684
ISBN 0-395-32936-1

Printed in the United States of America

H 10 9 8 7 6 5 4 3 2 1

The manuscript of *Mr. Bliss* is owned by Marquette University, Milwaukee, Wisconsin. The manuscript is held in the Department of Special Collections and University Archives. The publishers gratefully acknowledge the assistance of Marquette University in the publication of this work.

Mr. Bliss.

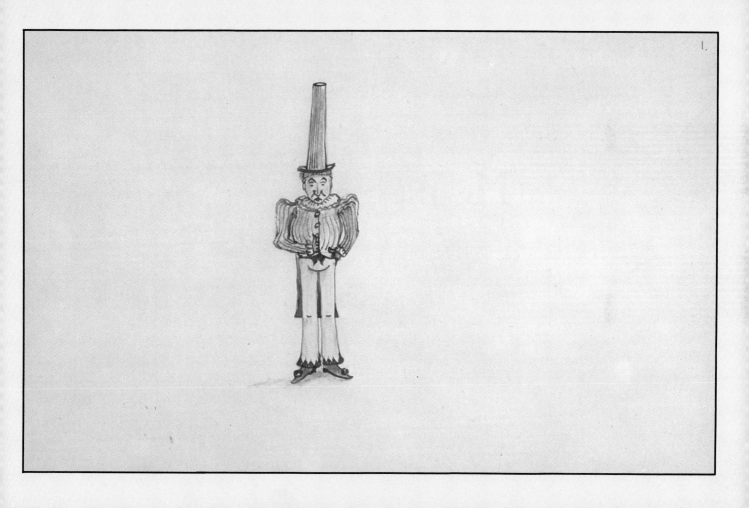

Mr. Bliss —

Mr. Bliss

lived in a house. It was a white house with red roofs. It had
tall rooms, and a very high front door, because Mr. Bliss wore such
tall hats. He had rows of them on rows of pegs in the hall.

lived in a house.   It was a white house with red roofs.   It had tall rooms, and a very high front door, because Mr. Bliss wore such tall hats.   He had rows of them on rows of pegs in the hall.

One day Mr. Bliss looked out of the window early in the morning.

"Is it going to be a fine day?" he asked the Girabbit (which he kept in the garden, but its head often looked in at the bedroom windows).

"Of course it is!" said the Girabbit. All days were fine to him for his skin was of mackintosh, and he had made a deep, deep, hole in the ground, and he was blind, so he never knew whether the sun was shining or not. As a matter of fact he usually went to bed after breakfast and got up for supper, so that he knew very little about the daytime.

One day Mr. Bliss looked out of the window early in the morning.
"Is it going to be a fine day?" he asked the girabbit (which he kept in the garden, but its head often looked in at the bedroom windows).

"Of course it is!" said the girabbit. All days were fine to it, for its skin was of mackintosh, and he had made a deep, deep, hole in the ground, and he was blind, so he never knew whether the sun was shining or not. As a matter of fact he usually went to bed after breakfast and got up for supper, so that he knew very little about the daytime.

After breakfast Mr. Bliss put on his green top-hat, because the Girabbit said it was going to be a fine day.

Then he said: "I will go and buy a motor-car!"

So he got on his bicycle, and rode down the hill to the village.

He walked into the shop, and said: "I want a motor-car!"

After breakfast Mr Bliss put on his green top-hat, because the girabbit said it was going to be a fine day.

Then he said "I will go and buy a motor-car!"

So he got on his bicycle, and rode down the hill to the village.

He walked into the shop, and said: "I want a motor-car!"

"What colour?" said Mr. Binks. "Bright yellow," said Mr. Bliss, "inside and out."

"That will be five shillings," said Mr. Binks.

"And I want red wheels," said Mr. Bliss.

"That will be sixpence more."

"Very well," said Mr. Bliss; "only I have left my purse at home."

"Very well, then you will have to leave your bicycle here; and when you bring your money you can have it back."

It was a beautiful bicycle, all silver — but it had no pedals, because Mr. Bliss only rode down hill.

"What colour?" said Mr. Binks.   "Bright yellow", said Mr. Bliss, "inside and out".

"That will be five shillings", said Mr. Binks.

"And I want red wheels" said Mr. Bliss.

"That will be sixpence more".

"Very well" said Mr. Bliss; "only I have left my purse at home".

"Very well, then you will have to leave your bicycle here; and when you bring your money you can have it back".

It was a beautiful bicycle, all silver —— but it had no pedals, because Mr. Bliss only rode down hill.

Mr. Bliss's motor-car.

Mr. Bliss got into the motor-car and started off. Soon he asked himself:

"Where are you going to, Mr. Bliss?"

"I don't know, Mr. Bliss," he answered himself.

"Let's go and visit the Dorkinses, and give them a surprise!"

"Very well!" said Mr. Bliss to himself, "very well!"

Mr Bliss's motor car.

Mr. Bliss got into the motor car and started off. Soon he asked himself:
"Where are you going to Mr. Bliss?"
"I don't know, Mr. Bliss," he answered himself.
"Let's go and visit the Dorkinses, and give them a surprise!"
"Very well!" said Mr. Bliss to himself, "very well!"

So he turned sharp to the right at the next turning, and ran straight into Mr. Day, coming from his garden with a barrow-load of cabbages. This shows what happened.

So he turned sharp to the right at the next turning, and ran straight into Mr. Day, coming from his garden with a barrow-load of cabbages. This shows what happened.

So he had to pick up Mr. Day and put the cabbages on the back of the motor-car. Mr. Day said he was too bruised to walk.

Now he went on again and turned sharp round the second turning to the left, and ran slap into Mrs. Knight with her donkey-cart piled with bananas.

The cart was smashed. So he had to pile the bananas on top of the cabbages, and Mrs. Knight on top of Mr. Day, and tie the donkey on behind the car.

So he had to pick up Mr. Day and put the cabbages on the back of the motor car.   M<u>r</u> Day said he was too bruised to walk.

Now he went on again, and turned sharp round the second turning to the left, and ran slap into M<u>rs</u> Knight with her donkey-cart piled with bananas

The cart was smashed.   So he had to pile the bananas on top of the cabbages, and M<u>rs</u> Knight on top of Mr. Day, and tie the donkey on behind the car.

The car was now very full, and would not go very fast. Soon they came into the wood, because the road ran through the middle of it.

The Car was now very full, and would not go very fast.   Soon they came
into the wood, because the road ran through the middle of it.

The Three
Bears' Wood.

Of course the bears came out, and stood in the middle of the road and waved their arms:
Archie and Teddy and Bruno.

ARCHIE   TEDDY   BRUNO

Of course the bears came out, and stood in the middle of the road and waved their arms: Archie and Teddy and Bruno.

ARCHIE   TEDDY   BRUNO

So Mr. Bliss had to stop, because he could not get by without running over them.

"I like bananas," said Teddy.

"And I like cabbages," said Archie.

"And I want a donkey!" said Bruno.

"And we all want a motor-car," they all said together.

"But you can't have this motor-car; it's mine," said Mr. Bliss.

"And you can't have these cabbages — they're mine," said Mr. Day.

"And you can't have these bananas, or this donkey — they're mine," said Mrs. Knight.

"Then we shall eat you all up — one each!" said the bears.

Of course they were only teasing; but they rolled their yellow eyes, and growled, and looked so fierce that Mr. Bliss was frightened (and so was Mr. Day and Mrs. Knight). So they gave the bears the cabbages and the bananas.

Archie and Teddy piled them on the donkey and took them away to their house in the wood. Bruno sat and talked to Mr. Bliss. Really he was watching to see Mr. Bliss did not drive away before Archie and Teddy came back.

So Mr. Bliss had to stop, because he could not get by without running over them.

"I like bananas", said Teddy.

"And I like cabbages", said Archie.

"And I want a donkey!", said Bruno.

"And we all want a motor-car", they all said together.

"But you can't have this motor-car; it's mine", said Mr. Bliss.

"And you can't have these cabbages — they're mine", said Mr. Day.

"And you can't have these bananas, or this donkey — they're mine", said Mr. Knight.

"Then we shall eat you all up — one each!", said the bears.

Of course they were only teasing; but they rolled their yellow eyes, and growled, and looked so fierce that Mr. Bliss was frightened (and so was Mr. Day and Mr. Knight). So they gave the bears the cabbages and the bananas.

Archie and Teddy piled them on the donkey and took them away to their house in the wood. Bruno sat and talked to Mr. Bliss. Really he was watching to see Mr. Bliss did not drive away before Archie and Teddy came back.

When they came back the bears said: "Now we want a motor-ride!"

"But I am going to see the Dorkinses," said Mr. Bliss, "and you don't know them."

"But we could know them," said Archie.

So Mr. Bliss had to let them all get in at the back, and there was such a squash that Mrs. Knight had to sit in front by Mr. Bliss, and he was so squeezed he could hardly steer.

Then they started off again, and came out of the Wood to the top of the Hill, because the road ran straight up it and down the other side.

Mr. Bliss's motor-car is drawn both going up the hill and rushing down the other side.

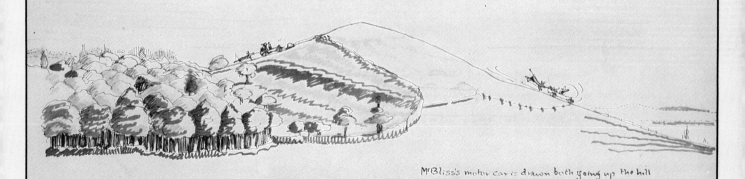

When they came back the bears said: " Now we want a motor-ride!"
" But I am going to see the Dorkinses", said Mr. Bliss, " and you don't know them".
" But we could know them", said Archie.

So Mr. Bliss had to let them all get in at the back; and there was such a squash that Mrs. Knight had to sit in front by Mr. Bliss, and he was so squeezed he could hardly steer.

Then they started off again, and came out of the Wood to the top of the Hill, because the road ran straight up it and down the other side.

Mr. Bliss's motor car is drawn both going up the hill and rushing down the other side.

The poor donkey was tied on behind again. He did not much mind at first because with six inside the motor did not go very fast up hill. But when they came to the top of the Hill, and began to go down (because the Dorkinses lived at the bottom) it was very different. Mr. Bliss was so squeezed by Mrs. Knight he could not put on the brakes. Soon they began to whizz and the Donkey was dragged flying through the air. Faster and faster they ran, until they crashed plump into the Dorkinses' garden wall. They all shot out head first and flew over the wall, all except the donkey, who turned a somersault into the car. Like this: ——————— .

The cabbages and bananas are not in the picture, of course — the bears had hidden them all in the Wood.

The poor donkey was tied on behind again. He did not much mind at first, because with six inside the motor did not go very fast up hill. But when they came to the top of the hill, and began to go down (because the Dorkinses lived at the bottom) it was very different. Mr. Bliss was so squeezed by Mr. Knight he could not put on the brakes. Soon they began to whizz and the Donkey was dragged flying through the air. Faster and faster they ran, until they crashed plump into the Dorkinses' garden wall. They all shot out head first, and flew over the wall, all except the donkey, who turned a somersault into the car. Like this:——————.

The cabbages and bananas are not in the picture, ~~talking while in the picture~~, of course — the bears had hidden them all in the Wood.

The Dorkinses

were the other side of the wall, sitting on their beautiful lawn on little stools. They were eating soup out of little bowls, and their lovely carpet was spread on the grass. They were fat people; but one of them was specially fat; and he

The Dorkinses

were the other side of the wall, sitting on their beautiful lawn on little stools.
They were eating soup out of little bowls, and their lovely carpet was spread on
the grass. They were fat people; but one of them was specially fat, and he

was known as the Fat Dorkins (or just Fattie). He had curly black hair, and wore no coat, because he split coats, when he tried to get into them. So he went about in a white shirt with yellow spots and no sleeves. The second fattest Dorkins (who was called Albert) is on the left; his legs were very short. Herbert is the one on the far side of the soup-tureen. He looks so horrified because he has just swallowed a beetle that got into his soup. Egbert is the one with a green jacket. He also looks cross, because there is another beetle on the lovely carpet (you can see he is just going to smack it with his spoon). But Albert looked much more horrified a second later, and the beetle was squashed very flat. Not by Egbert! It was just then that Mr. Bliss and all his party fell out of the sky onto the Dorkinses, the soup, the beetle, and the lovely carpet.

was known as the Fat Dorkins (or just Fattie). He had curly black hair; and wore no coat, because he split coats, when he tried to get into them. So he went about in a shite shirt with yellow spots and no sleeves. The second fattest Dorkins (who was called Albert) is on the left; his legs were very short. Herbert is the one on the far side of the soup-tureen. He looks so horrified, because he has just swallowed a beetle that got into his soup. Egbert is the one with a green jacket. He also looks cross, because there is another beetle on the lovely carpet. (you can see he is just going to smack it with his spoon). But Albert looked much more horrified a second later, and the beetle was squashed very flat. Not by Egbert! It was just then that Mr. Bliss and all his party fell out of the sky onto the Dorkinses, the soup, the beetle, and the lovely carpet.

Mr. Bliss fell face downwards on the beetle. Mr. Day knocked Albert over and stood on his head on the lovely carpet. Bruno sat down bump. Teddy sat on Herbert. Mrs. Knight sent Egbert over backwards. But Archie put his head bang through the lid of the tureen, and soup splashed all over him, and got into both his eyes.

The Dorkinses were quite bowled over — and angry. Fattie was least angry, because nobody had fallen on him. Though he lost his third helping of soup, he laughed very loud. That only made Albert all the angrier.

"Next time you come," he said to Mr. Bliss, "go to the front door and ring, and don't throw people out of a balloon onto our picnic!"

"We didn't come in a balloon — I brought my friends in a motor-car, and we left it at the gate."

"Thank goodness," said Egbert. "A motor-car on the lovely carpet would have been too much to bear. I believe one of your friends is sitting on a beetle."

Then Mrs. Knight jumped up with a shriek, although she had been lying on her back crying "O my bananas — all my bones are broken!" She would not sit down, till Mr. Bliss showed her the beetle squashed on his front. By that time Archie had licked himself clean of soup; Mr. Day had found his hat, and was sitting up again; and Bruno (who was

Archie,
I mean /

Mr. Bliss fell face downwards on the beetle. Mr. Day knocked Albert over and stood on his head on the lovely carpet. Bruno sat down bump. ~~Archie~~ sat on Herbert. Mr. Knight sent Egbert over backwards. But ~~Teddy~~ put his head bang through the lid of the tureen, and soup splashed all over him, and got into both his eyes

The Dorkinses were quite bowled over — and angry, angry, because nobody had fallen on him. Though he lost of soup, he laughed very loud. That only made Albert all

'Next time you come,' he said to Mr. Bliss, 'go to the front and don't throw people out of a balloon onto our picnic!"

Fattie was least
his third helping
the angrier.
door and ring;

' We didn't come in a balloon — I brought my friends in a motor-car; and we left it at the gate'.

'Thank goodness' said Egbert. 'A motor-car on the lovely carpet would have been too much to bear. I believe one of your friends is sitting on a beetle".

Then Mr. Knight jumped up with a shriek, although she had been lying on her back crying 'O my bananas — all my bones are broken!' She would not sit down, till Mr. Bliss showed her the beetle squashed on his front. By that time ~~Teddy~~ Archie had licked himself clean of soup; Mr. Day had found his hat, and was sitting up again; and Bruno (who was very little) was picking daisies. So Mr. Bliss introduced them all to the Dorkinses, and the Dorkinses, who were very polite, said: "Pleased to meet you, we hope you are quite well. Isn't it lovely weather, and won't you stay to lunch." They did not really mean any of it very much (except the part about the weather — for the Girabbit had, by accident, been quite right). But Mr. Bliss and Mrs. Knight said: "Thank you very much." And the bears said: "We would rather walk round your beautiful garden, if you don't mind." So lots more soup was brought out, and cakes, and pickled cabbage and banana-fritters, and they all sat on the grass and ate. Except the bears who disappeared.

After lunch they walked round the garden. There was no sign of the bears, till they came to the kitchen-garden.

This is just a glimpse of what they saw there.

The three bears fast asleep under a large apple-tree.

They were snoring and their tummies were frightfully fat.

There was only one little row of cabbages left in all the great big garden.

The bears had eaten all the rest, and lots of green apples, and raw potatoes.

very little) was picking daisies.   So Mr. Bliss introduced them all to the Dorkinses, and the Dorkinses, who were very polite, said: 'Pleased to meet you; we hope you are quite well. Isn't it lovely weather, and won't you stay to lunch'.   They did not really mean any of it very much (except the part about the weather — for the girabbit had, by accident, been quite right). But Mr. Bliss and Mr. Knight said: 'Thank you, very much'.   And the bears said 'we would rather walk round your beautiful garden, if you don't mind'.   So lots more soup was brought out, and cakes, and pickled cabbage and banana-fritters, and they all sat on the grass and ate. Except the bears, who disappeared.

After lunch they walked round the garden. There was no sign of the bears, till they came to the kitchen-garden.

This is just a glimpse of what they saw there.
The three bears fast asleep under a large apple-tree.

They were snoring, and their tummies were frightfully fat.

There was only one little row of cabbages left in all the great big garden.

The bears had eaten all the rest, and lots of green apples, and raw potatoes.

The Dorkinses were really and truly angry this time, because Archie had not even left the purple cabbages they used for pickling.

So they shook the bears, and woke them up, and told them to go away at once.

"What nasty cross people your friends are, Mr. Bliss," said Archie. "They ask you to lunch and then are angry if you eat it. We are going to finish our nap."

They all lay down under the tree again and would not move. But the crossest Dorkins, Albert, let loose the dogs.

The Dorkinses were really and truly angry this time, because Archie had not even left the purple cabbages they used for pickling.

So they shook the bears, and woke them up,  and told them to go away at once.

'What nasty cross peeple your friends are, Mr. Bliss' said Archie. 'They ask you to lunch and then are angry if you eat it. We are going to finish our nap.'

They all lay down under the tree again and would not move. But the crossest Dorkins, Albert, let loose the dogs.

Then the bears woke up very suddenly and scrambled over the wall and ran away as hard as their legs would carry them. Luckily for them the gates were all shut, and the Dorkinses did not let the dogs into the road.

"Never mind," they called back, "we have got lots of cabbages and bananas at home."

Then the bears woke up very suddenly and scrambled over the wall and ran away as hard as their legs would carry them. Luckily for them the gates were all shut, and the Dorkinses did not let the dogs into the road.

"Never mind", they called back, "we have got lots of cabbages _and_ bananas at home""

"My cabbages!" shouted Mr. Day.

"My bananas!" shrieked Mrs. Knight. "Drat the bears; I am a-going after them!"

"But they will eat you all up," said Mr. Bliss; "and anyway you will never catch them up now."

"They will eat the cabbages and bananas all up, you mean," said Mr. Day. "We shall easily catch them up in the motor-car."

"No!" said Mr. Bliss. "I am not going to chase bears. I would rather let them eat bananas than me."

"That's because they ain't your bananas," said Mrs. Knight. And they pushed Mr. B. towards the gate.

'My cabbages!', shouted Mr Day.

'My bananas!' shrieked Mrs. Knight. 'Drat the bears; I am a-going after them!'

'But they will eat you all up', said Mr. Bliss; 'and anyway you will never catch them up now'.

'They will eat the cabbages and bananas all up, you mean', said Mr. Day. 'We shall easily catch them up in the motor-car'.

'No!' said Mr. Bliss, 'I am not going to chase bears. I would rather let them eat bananas than me'.

'That's because they ain't your bananas', said Mr. Knight. And they pushed Mr. B. towards the gate

But they could not get him through! Still they pushed and squeezed him against the posts, until at last he said he would go after the bears, if the Dorkinses came too, and brought the dogs. The Dorkinses rather liked the idea, for they were still angry with the bears. But, of course, when they got to the motor-car, the Dorkinses saw at once that it would not go again without a lot of mending.

"What are we to do?" said Mr. Bliss. "This car is worth five and sixpence, and Binks has got my silver bicycle!"

"Hee-haw! Hee-haw!" said the donkey suddenly from behind a hedge. They had forgotten all about him, and he had gone to find his own lunch — thistles.

"I know!" said Mr. Bliss, immediately he heard the donkey — "the donkey shall pull the car home."

"No he won't," said Mrs. Knight, "not if I knows him."

She knew him quite well. He was already trotting away quickly. They shouted, and shouted, and offered him four pounds of carrots. So at last he stopped and waited to see what would happen next.

But they could not get him through! Still they pushed and squeezed him against the posts, until at last he said he would go after the bears, if the Dorkinses came too, and brought the dogs. The Dorkinses rather liked the idea, for they were still angry with the bears. But, of course, when they got to the motor-car, the Dorkinses saw at once that it would not go again without a lot of mending.

"What are we to do?" said Mr. Bliss. "This car is worth five and sixpence, and Binks has got my silver bicycle!"

"Hee-haw! Hee-haw!" said the donkey suddenly from behind a hedge. They had forgotten all about him, and he had gone to find his own lunch — thistles.

"I know," said Mr. Bliss, immediately he heard the donkey, — "the donkey shall pull the car home."

"No he won't", said Mrs. Knight, "not if I knows him".

She knew him quite well. He was already trotting away quickly. They shouted, and shouted, and offered him four pounds of carrots. So at last he stopped and waited to see what would happen next.

You can guess what did! They brought out carrots, and coaxed the donkey back. And then they tied him up. Then they fetched out three ponies (Albert's, Egbert's, and Herbert's — Fattie was too heavy to have a pony). Then they tied all the ponies and the donkey on to the front of the car, after they had hammered and banged the wheels straight, and after that they all got in: Mr. Bliss, Mr. Day, Mrs. Knight, Albert, Herbert, Egbert, and Fattie, and the dogs, who couldn't be trusted not to go off after rabbits.

You can guess what did! They brought out carrots, and coaxed the donkey back.
And then they tied him up. Then they fetched out three ponies (Albert's, Egbert's, and
Herbert's — Fattie was too heavy to have a pony). Then they tied all the ponies and the
donkey on to the front of the car, after they had hammered and banged the wheels straight,
and after that they all got in: <u>Mr. Bliss</u>, <u>Mr. Day</u>, <u>Mrs. Knight</u>, <u>Albert</u>, <u>Herbert</u>, <u>Egbert</u>, <u>and</u>
<u>Fattie</u>, <u>and</u> the dogs. She couldn't be trusted not to go off after rabbits.

Just as they were starting Fattie said: "It will be tea-time long before we get there. Let's wait till after tea, or have an early tea now!" But they wouldn't listen to him. Anyway it was too much bother to unpack themselves all over again.

It took them much longer than they expected getting up the long long hill. And it took them still longer going down the other side, because they had to keep the brakes on, or the car would have run away and pushed the ponies and the donkey over. It was already very late tea-time when they got to the inn at Cross Roads. Then Fattie insisted on stopping. They had a huge tea, especially Fattie. They had no money, so the innkeeper made out a huge bill for Mr. Bliss — the Dorkinses said it was his party.

I have drawn a picture of the party on the inn-green by the road side. The car is just here (and the ponies and donkey) but I am tired of drawing it.

Just as they were starting Fattie said : "It will be tea-time long before we get there. Let's wait till after tea, or have an early tea now!" But they would'nt listen to him. Anyway it was too much bother to unpack themselves all over again.

It took them much longer than they expected getting up the long long hill. And it took them still longer going down the other side, because they had to keep the brakes on, or the car would have run away and pushed the ponies and the donkey over. It was already very late tea-time when they got to the inn at Cross Roads. Then Fattie insisted on stopping. They had a huge tea, especially Fattie. They had no money, so the innkeeper made out a huge bill for Mr Bliss — the Dorkinses said it was his party.

I have drawn a picture of the party on the inn-green by the road side. The car is just here (and the ↓ ponies

O

and donkey) but I am tired of drawing it.

DORKIN

When Fattie had finished at last, they packed themselves up and started.

It is a good way from Cross Roads to Three Bears Wood. Very soon the sun began to sink. Dark was coming on and the moon was rising when they came to the edge of the Wood.

Even Mrs. Knight began to wonder whether her bananas were worth all the trouble, when she saw how bluey-dark the wood could look. She thought "the dogs will look after us!" But the dogs thought: "It is one thing to chase bears out of the garden in the afternoon, and quite a different thing to hunt them in their own wood after dark. Where are our nice comfy kennels?"

Albert said: "Isn't it time you put on your lamps?"

Then Mr. Bliss remembered he had never bought any — as you will see if you look back at the pictures. He had only bothered about the colour of the wheels.

"Never mind," said Herbert. "There won't be any policeman out in this lonely place."

"I wish there were," said Mr. Bliss — "lots and lots of policemen."

When Fattie had finished at last, they packed themselves up and started.

It is a good way from Cross Roads to Three Bears wood. Very soon the sun began to sink. Dark was coming on, and the moon was rising when they came to the edge of the Wood.

Even Mrs. Knight bananas were worth bluey-dark the "the dogs will look "It is one thing to afternoon, and in their own wood comfy kennels?".

Albert said: "Is'nt Then Mr. Bliss any — as you will see He had only bothered

began to wonder whether her all the trouble, when she saw how wood could look. She thought after us!". But the dogs thought: chase bears out of the garden in the quite a different thing to hunt them after dark. Where are our nice

it time you put on your lamps?" remembered he had never bought if you look back at the pictures. about the colour of the wheels.

"Never mind" said Herbert. "There wont be any policeman out in this lonely place".

"I wish there were", said Mr. Bliss — "lots and lots of policemen".

They drove only just inside the wood, and dragged the car off the road. Then they tied up the ponies and donkey, and set off. The dogs were leading, because they smelt bear, and Albert Dorkins would not let them run away, but Mr. Bliss was behindmost, and he probably would have never come along, if he had not hated being left alone. Anyway Mrs. Knight kept on looking back to see he was following. The wood got darker and darker as they went deeper and deeper. All they could see was the faint signs of a path — the path the bears made going to and from their house.

Then the path got wider, and became a road. So they walked very slow and quiet.

Mr. Bliss sat down and thought he would wait till they came back.

This is all he could see. He did not like it [at] all. "I can't see if my hat is black or green," he said.

"I know your face is white without looking," said Mrs. K., who was only just in front. "You come along with the rest!" So Mr. Bliss had to come along. Not much further. They were very near the bears' house now. As a matter of fact, it stood just round a corner at the back of the picture, which Albert has nearly reached.

They drove only just inside the wood, and dragged the car off the road. Then they tied up the ponies and donkey, and set off. The dogs were leading, because they smelt bear, and Albert Dorkins would not let them run away; but Mr Bliss was behindmost, and he probably would have never come along, if he had not hated being left alone. Anyway Mr Knight kept on looking back to see he was following. The wood got darker and darker as they went deeper and deeper. All they could see was the faint signs of a path — the path the bears made going to and from their house.

Then the path got wider, and became a road. So they walked very slow and quiet. Mr Bliss sat down and thought he would wait till they came back.

This is all he could see. He did not like it all. "I can't see if my hat is black or green" he said. "I know your

face is white without looking" said Mr K., who was only just in front. "You come along with the rest!" So Mr Bliss had to come along. Not much further. They were very near the bears' house now. As a matter of fact, it stood just round a corner at the back of the picture, which Albert has nearly reached.

The dogs went round the corner. Suddenly they gave the most dreadful howls, and bolted back with their tails between their legs and their hair on end. Mr. Bliss did not wait to see what they had seen, but fled after them as fast as his long legs would carry him. Every time he bumped into a tree he got more frightened, and every time he tripped up and fell flat on his nose he got up and ran faster without ever looking back. He forgot motor-car, ponies, cabbages, Dorkinses and all, and ran all night till morning. But in the meanwhile, you would like to see what the dogs saw — and the Dorkinses and Mrs. Knight, and Mr. Day. They did not turn to run away until it was too late.

Now, are you surprised that they all lay down on the ground and hid their faces — even Albert?

How did the bears do it? That is their own private secret. I expect they painted themselves with something that shines in the dark, and that they had been expecting the people to come after them. I expect that, as soon as they heard the dogs snuffling outside their house (which you can see), they popped out. But I don't think they expected to

29

The dogs went round the corner. Suddenly they gave the most dreadful howls, and bolted back with their tails between their legs and their hair on end. Mr. Bliss did not wait to see what they had seen, but fled after them as fast as his long legs would carry him. Every time he bumped into a tree he got more frightened, and every time he tripped up and fell flat on his nose he got up and ran faster without ever looking back. He forgot motor-car, ponies, cabbages, Dorkinses and all, and ran all night till morning. But in the meanwhile, you would like to see what the dogs saw — and the Dorkinses and Mr. Bright, and Mr. Day. They didn't turn to run away until it was too late.

Now, are you down on the ground Albert?.

How did the bears private secret.

surprised that they all lay and hid their faces — even

do it?. That is their own I expect they painted themselves with something that shines in the dark, and that they had been expecting the people to come after them. I expect that, as soon as they heard the dogs snuffling outside their house (which you can see), they popped out. But I don't think they expected to frighten

frighten everybody as much as they did. The people thought they were bogies, or ghosts, or goblins, or all three. Fattie rolled on the floor. So did Mrs. Knight, and she kept on saying "bananas, bananas, bananas", as if she was counting. Mr. Day hid his face in his hat, and said "I will be good, I will be good." The other Dorkinses lay as quiet and as still as they could for shaking.

Then the bears began to laugh. They did laugh! They sat on the floor and roared, and when they got up again they left shiny patches like enormous glowworms on the ground.

"Now we had better all have supper," said Archie, when he got his breath. Herbert was the first to recover, and he was cross, because he felt so silly. But when Fattie heard "supper", he forgot all his troubles.

The bears really took pains with that supper, and the Dorkinses and Mrs. Knight and old Mr. Day forgave them altogether when they saw it; and when they had eaten it they danced and sang together like old friends. But they couldn't find Mr. Bliss anywhere, though they roused all the birds with their calling and shouting, before they sat down. There is a picture of the party on the other side.

everybody as much as they did. The people thought they were bogies, or ghosts, or goblins, or all three. Fattie rolled on the floor. So did Mrs. Knight, and she kept on saying "bananas, bananas, bananas", as if she was counting. Mr. Day hid his face in his hat, and said "I will be good, I will be good". The other Dorkinses lay as quiet and as still as they could for shaking.

Then the bears began to laugh. They did laugh! They sat on the floor and roared; and when they got up again they left shiny patches like enormous glowworms on the ground.

"Now we had better all have supper", said Archie, when he got his breath. Herbert was the first to recover, and he was cross, because he felt so silly. But when Fattie heard "supper", he forgot all his troubles.

The bears really took pains with that supper, and the Dorkinses and Mrs. Knight and old Mr. Day forgave them altogether when they saw it; and when they had eaten it they danced and sang together like old friends. But they couldn't find Mr. Bliss anywhere, though they roused all the birds in the trees, calling and shouting, before they sat down. There is a picture of the party on the other side.

This is at the end of the party when nearly everything had been eaten — cold chicken, ham, lettuces, beetroot, tomatoes, trifle, cheese, brown bread, and asparagus — the birthday cake (it wasn't anybody's birthday, really) is still left, but the beer-barrel is very nearly empty.

Mr. Day is telling a story, and Mrs. Knight is pretending not to listen. Bruno and Fattie are too full to do anything except sit quiet.

It was very late before they finished, and very late indeed when they had washed up. Of course it was too late to go home. So the bears

Herbert is not in this picture. He swallowed a crumb the wrong way and is coughing in the scullery. He was sitting beyond Egbert next to Teddy.

31

Herbert is not
in this picture.
He swallowed
a crumb the
wrong way &
is coughing in
the scullery.
He __was__ sitting
beyond Egbert
next to Teddy

This is at the end of the party
when nearly everything had been eaten —
cold chicken, ham, lettuce, beet-root,
tomatoes, trifle, cheese, brown bread,
and asparagus — the birthday cake
(it wasn't anybody's birthday, really)
is still left, but the beer-barrel is
very nearly empty.
Mr. Day is telling a story, and Mrs.
Knight is pretending not to listen.
Bruno and Fattie are too full to
do anything except sit quiet.

It was very late before they finished,
and very late indeed when they had
washed up.   Of course it was
too late to go home. So the bears

invited them to stay the night. Imagine staying all night in the Bears' House — but they all felt quite friendly at this time, and no one mentioned either cabbages or bananas, nor did anyone ask the bears where they got their excellent food (the bears were generally supposed not to pay for anything, but to get it by 'prowling' — in fact they were rascals, though they could be very jolly at supper).

The bears had quite a large house, long and low, with no upstairs. Herbert and Egbert slept in the double spare-bed and everyone found some sort of bed — except Fattie. None of the beds would bear him. So he slept by the fire, on a mattress and cushions, and snored happily all night. Perhaps he dreamed he was a kettle on the hob. The ponies and donkey were fetched too, and put in one of the bears' big outhouses. So everyone was comfortable.

And they woke early next morning, and then the story went on.

invited them to stay the night.   Imagine staying all night in the Bears' House — but they all felt quite friendly at this time, and no one mentioned either cabbages or bananas, nor did any one ask the bears where they got their excellent food (the bears were generally supposed not to pay for anything, but to get it by 'prowling' — in fact they were rascals, though they could be every jolly at supper).

The Bears had quite a large house, long and low, with no upstairs.

Herbert and Egbert slept in the double spare-bed, and every one found some sort of bed — except Fattie. None of the beds would bear him. So he slept by

the fire, on a mattress and cushions, and snored happily all night. Perhaps he dreamed he was a kettle on the hob.   The ponies and donkey were ~~the~~ fetched too, and put in one of the bears' big out-houses. So everyone was comfortable.

And they woke early next-morning, and then the story went on.

What happened to Mr. Bliss? He ran all night without knowing where he was running to, jumping over hedges, falling into ditches, tearing his clothes on barbed wire. When dawn came he was dead tired, and he found himself sitting on the top of a hill. He ought to have been miles and miles away, but he was looking down into his own village and could see his own house in the distance on a further hill.

"There is either a flag flying from my chimney or else the sweep has got in — though I never ordered him to come," he said to himself.

33.

What happened to Mr. Bliss?   He ran all night without knowing where he was running to, jumping over hedges, falling into ditches, tearing his clothes on barbed wire.   When dawn came he was dead tired, and he found himself sitting on the top of a hill.   He ought to have been miles and miles away, but he was looking down into his own village and could see his own house in the distance on a further hill.

" There is either a flag flying from my chimney or else the sweep has got in —— though I never ordered him to come " he said to himself.

"Well, I am blessed!" said Mr. Bliss aloud, and he got up and staggered down hill, over fields and fences, till he struck the road through the village. He went to Binks's, but no one was up. So he pushed into the yard at the side of the shop, and there was his bicycle just inside a shed. He wheeled it out, and started home.

Of course he meant to come sailing down the hill again with his purse as soon as he had changed his clothes and put on his shopping hat (and had some breakfast). But you will agree it looked most suspicious. So thought Mr. Binks peeping through his bedroom window. He began to dress in a great rage, long before his usual time. "All right, my lad," said he, "I'll go straight to

34

"Well, I am blessed!" said Mr. Bliss, aloud, and he got up and staggered down hill, over fields and fences, till he struck the road through the village.   He went to Binks's, but noone was up.   So he pushed into the yard at the side of the shop, and there was his bicycle just inside a shed.   He wheeled it out, and started home.

Of course he meant to come sailing down the hill again with his purse as soon as he had changed his clothes and put on his shopping hat (and had some breakfast). But you will agree it looked most suspicious.   So thought Mr. Binks peeping through his bedroom window.   He began to dress in a great rage, long before his usual time.   "All right, my lad," said he, "I'll go straight to

Sergeant Boffin at the police station, and he'll learn you to go off with my motor-cars, and never bring 'em back.'' All the same he did not put off breakfast, nor did he hurry over it. While he was munching a sausage, and wondering how Mr. Bliss would like to spend his summer holidays in prison, away in the Bears' House there was a lot of talking.

The bears were in a very good temper that morning. They gave back Mrs. Knight her bananas (or most of them); they gave Mr. Day some fresh cabbages (and he did not ask where they got them). But Mrs. Knight wanted a new cart, and Mr. Day wanted a new

35

Sergeant Boffin at the police-station, and he'll learn you to go off with my motor-cars, and never bring 'em back". All the same he did not put off breakfast, nor did he hurry over it. While he was munching a sausage, and wondering how Mr. Bliss would like to spend his summer-holidays in prison, away in the Bear's House there was a lot of talking.

[This is a lifelike portrait of Sergeant Boffin without his helmet]

The Bears were in a very good temper that morning. They gave back Mr. Knight her bananas (or most of them); they gave Mr. Day some fresh cabbages (and he did not ask where they got them). But Mr. Knight wanted a new cart, and Mr. Day wanted a new barrow, and the Dorkinses wanted a new soup-tureen, and the bears wanted some fun; and each of them thought Mr. Bliss was the man to get it from. Also the Dorkinses suddenly thought they might charge Mr. Bliss for hire of ponies — which was not nice of them, as they were disgustingly rich.

Anyway after an early breakfast they all started off again together. It was a great squash of course, because although Mr. B. had run goodness knows where, and the dogs had run home, the bears and the Dorkinses and the other two made nine. Bruno sat on Mrs. Knight's lap, and Archie and Teddy took up as much room as they could — but Fattie did not leave much.

When they got to the village, they found a row going on — or just beginning. Mr. Binks was trying to make Sergeant Boffin believe that Mr. Bliss was a thief, and that he ought to run straight up the hill barrow, and the Dorkinses wanted a new soup-tureen, and the bears wanted some fun; and each of them thought Mr. Bliss was the man to get it from. Also the Dorkinses suddenly thought they might charge Mr. Bliss for hire of ponies — which was not nice of them, as they were disgustingly rich.

Anyway after an early breakfast they all started off again together. It was a great squash of course, 'cause although Mr. B. had run goodness knows where, and the dogs had run home, the bears and the Dorkinses and the other two made nine. Bruno sat on Mr. Knight's lap, and Archie and Teddy took up as much room as they could — but Fattie did not leave much.

When they got to the village, they found a row going on — or just beginning. Mr. Binks was trying to make Sergeant Boffin believe that Mr. Bliss was a thief, and that he ought to run straight up the hill

and bring him back to prison. In the picture Sergeant Boffin is just saying: "Wot! 'im 'as lives up the 'ill''; and Binks is shouting, and people are coming out. You can see Sam, Sergeant Boffin's eldest boy, calling to his friends to come and see his dad knock old Binks down. The barber and the butcher are there; the cobbler (next door) is peeping; Uncle Joe is at the door with his specs on, Mrs. Golightly is standing with a parcel in her arm, and has stopped talking to Mrs. Simkins, old Gaffer Gamgee is trying hard to hear, elegant Alfred is taking a superior interest; there is somebody else's face at another window, and there are one or two kids.

But this is absolutely nothing to the excitement a minute later, when up rolled Mr. Binks' car, full of bears and Dorkinses and others, drawn by three ponies and a donkey. All the village was there in a minute. And they laughed. And they said things about Mr. Binks' tin-cars that made him angrier than he was before.

"He ought to be in prison he ought," said he, "sending home a nice car bent and all, and full of a parcel of bears and strange folk."

"G-r-r-r-r," said Archie; and Mr. Binks stepped back sudden[ly] and fell in the gutter.

"Now stand up and be polite, and say 'thank you'!" said Archie. "You ought to be very pleased we have bothered to bring your car back. Mr. Bliss left it in our wood, and ran away, and hasn't been seen since."

"O yes, 'e 'as," said Binks. "I seen him sneaking 'ome, early this morning, as I was a-telling the sergeant 'ere."

and bring him back to prison. In the picture Sergeant Boffin is just saying: "Wot! 'im as lives up the 'ill"; and Binks is shouting, and people are coming out. You can see Sam, Sergeant Boffin's eldest boy, calling to his friends to come and see his dad knock old Binks down. The barber, and the butcher are there; the cobbler (next-door) is peeping; Uncle Joe is at the door with his 'specs on, Mrs. Golightly is standing with a parcel on her arm, and has stopped talking to Mrs. Simkins; old Gaffer Gamgee is trying hard to hear; elegant Alfred is taking a superior interest; there is somebody else's face at another window, and there are one or two kids.

But this is absolutely nothing to the excitement a minute later, when up rolled Mr. Binks' car, full of bears and Dorkinses and others, drawn by three ponies and a donkey. All the village was there in a minute. And they laughed. And they said things about Mr. Binks' tin-cars that made him angrier than he was before.

"He ought to be in prison he ought", said he, "sending home a nice car bent and all, and full of a parcel of bears and strange folk."

"G—r—r—r—r" said Archie; and Mr. Binks stepped back sudden and fell in the gutter.

"Now stand up and be polite, and say 'thank-you'!" said Archie. "You ought to be very pleased we have bothered to bring your car back. Mr. Bliss left it in our wood, and ran away, and hasn't been seen since."

"O yes, 'e 'as", said Binks. "I seen him sneaking 'ome, early this morning, as I was a-telling the sergeant 'ere".

"Then we must follow him," said Teddy; "he owes money to everybody. Mr. Day wants a new barrow, Mrs. Knight wants a new cart, the Dorkinses want a new soup-tureen, Mr. Binks wants his money; and we want to see him too. We will all call together."

And that's what they decided to do. Poor Mr. Bliss knew nothing of all this. He was having fresh troubles. As soon as he got to the top of the hill (very tired) he looked up at his chimney. Then he stood still in the road.

"I am blessed and bothered," he said, "if it isn't the Girabbit's head sticking out of my chimney; and he seems to be munching carpet" (that's why he looked like a flag from far away).

"Then we must follow him", said Teddy; "he owes money to everybody. Mr Day wants a new barrow, Mrs Knight wants a new cart, the Dorkinses want a new soup-tureen, Mr Binks wants his money; and we want to see him too. We will all call together."

And thats what they decided to do. Poor Mr. Bliss knew nothing of all this. He was having fresh troubles. As soon as he got to the top of the hill (very tired) he looked up at his chimney. Then he stood still in the road.

"I am blessed and bothered", he said, "if it isn't the Girabbit's head sticking out of my chimney; and he seems to be munching carpet" (thats why he looked like a flag from far away).

It was the Girabbit's head! Mr. B. had gone off and forgotten to feed it, so it had burst open the back-door, squeezed in finally into the dining-room, and eaten its way through the ceiling into the best bedroom — and through the next ceiling into the attic, and up the attic chimney, knocking off the pots. There he was blinking in the morning sun with a large piece of the best-bedroom hearthrug in his mouth.

This will give you some idea of what Mr. Bliss saw when he got inside. Though he had had the Girabbit for some years, he was very surprised. He did not know that its neck was quite so telescopic.

Mr. Bliss was also really and truly angry; but the Girabbit would not come down again, not though Mr. B. pulled hard at his tail in the dining-room.

All he would do was to keep on saying "It's going to be a wet day! — leave me alone!"

Mr. B. was so tired that he left it alone, changed his clothes, took some food on the lawn, and had a kind of breakfast-lunch (or brunch).

Then he fell fast asleep, under a tree, and forgot even to dream.

Just after eleven he was waked up by the Girabbit speaking. "There's a powerful lot of people coming up the hill, Mr. Bliss," said he. "I can hear Sergeant Boffin's voice, and Binks's, and the voices of those Dorkinses you had to tea last Tuesday; and other folk; and bears growling."

It was the girabbit's head!   Mr. B. had gone off and forgotten to feed it, so it had burst open the back-door, squeezed in finally into the dining-room, and eaten its way through the ceiling into the best bedroom — and through the next ceiling into the attic, and up the attic chimney, knocking off the pots.   There he was blinking in the morning sun with a large piece of the best-bedroom hearthrug in his mouth.

This will give you some idea of what Mr. Bliss saw when he got inside. Though he had the Girabbit for some years, he was very surprised. He did not know that its neck was quite so telescopic. Mr. Bliss was also really and truly angry; but the girabbit would not come down again, not though Mr. B. pulled

hard at his tail in the dining-room. All he would do was to keep on saying "It's going to be a wet day — leave me alone!"

Mr. B. was so tired that he left it alone, changed his clothes, took some food on the lawn, and had a kind of breakfast - lunch (or brunch).

Then he fell fast asleep, under a tree, and forgot even to dream.

Just after eleven he was waked up by the girabbit speaking.   "There's a powerful lot of people coming up the hill, Mr. Bliss", said he.   "I can hear Sergeant Boffin's voice, and Binks's, and the voices of those Dorkinses you had to tea last Tuesday; and other folk; and bears growling."

(The Girabbit may be practically blind, but it can hear mighty sharp). "And they all seem dreadfully angry with you, Mr. Bliss," added the Girabbit.

"Lawks!" said Mr. Bliss; "What are they saying?"

"They are saying: we are going to take it out of old Bliss, and twice over, we are."

"Save us!" said Mr. Bliss, and darted indoors and shot all the bolts and turned all the keys.

Then he peeped out of a bedroom window, but the Girabbit pulled in his head.

Soon up came Boffin, and Binks, and the Dorkinses, and the bears, and Mrs. Knight, and Mr. Day, and lots of the people of the village.

There was no sign of the wet day the Girabbit spoke of.

It was hot, and they mopped their faces.

Then they all shouted: "Mr. BLISS!"

No answer.

So Mr. Binks shouted: "I wants my money." And they all shouted in chorus: "'E wants 'is money, and 'e means to 'ave it."

No answer.

"Why don't you arrest him?" said Archie, who was standing by the gate.

"I will!" said Boffin.

40

(The girrabbit may be practically blind, but it can hear mighty sharp). "And they all seem dreadfully angry with you, Mr. Bliss", added the girrabbit.

"Lawks!", said Mr. Bliss; "What are they saying?"

"They are saying: we are going to take it out of old Bliss, and twice over, we are".

"Save us!" said Mr. Bliss, and darted indoors and shot all the bolts and turned all the keys.

Then he peeped out of a bed-room window, but the girrabbit pulled in his head.

Soon up came Boffin, and Binks, and the Dorkinses, and the bears, and Mrs knight, and Mr. Day, and lots of the people of the village.

There was no sign of the vet-day the girrabbit spoke of. It was hot, and they mopped their faces.

Then they all shouted:

"Mr. BLISS!"

No answer.

So Mr. Binks shouted: "I wants my money". And they all shouted in chorus: "E wants is money, and e means to ave it".

No answer.

"Why don't you arrest him?" said Archie, who was standing by the gate.

"Tush!" said Boffin.

"Ha! ha! I see you," said the Girabbit at that second, popping his neck a yard or two out of the chimney. He heard them, not saw them, but they did not know that. They looked up and saw him, and that was enough. They were astonished. Indeed most of them fell flat on the spot. (You see Mr. Bliss had so far kept the Girabbit quite secret, because he did not want to pay Sergeant Boffin for a licence for keeping him, as he was sure it would be double price — quite 15/- a year. The Girabbit was trained to dive down a hole when strangers came up the hill and up to now no one else had seen more than his head. This day was an exception — because the Girabbit had quite forgotten where it was, and thought it was in its own hole!).

"Get up, get up!" squeaked the Girabbit. "Get up, and go away, or I shall come out of my hole and jump on you"; and in popped his head.

Then they got up and went (you can see them on the last page) — very quickly. All except the bears who were not particularly frightened. They went behind a hedge.

41

"Ha! ha! I see you" said the girabbit at that second, popping his neck a yard or two out of the chimney. He heard them, not saw them, but they did not know that. They looked up and saw him, and that was enough. They were astonished. Indeed most of them fell flat on the spot. (You see Mr. Bliss had so far kept the girabbit quite secret, 'cause he did not want to pay Sergeant Boffin for a licence for keeping him, as he was sure it would be double price — quite 15% a year). The girabbit was trained to dive down a hole when strangers come up the hill, and up to now no one else had seen more than his head. This day was an exception — because the girabbit had quite forgotten where it was, and thought it was in its own hole!).

"Getup, getup!" squeaked the girabbit. "Getup, and go away, or I shall come out of my hole and jump on you"; and in popped his head

Then they got up and went (you can see them on the last page) — very quickly. All except the bears who were not particularly frightened. They went behind a hedge.

The others fell over one another in their hurry. Fattie and Sergeant Boffin rolled over and over like barrels, quite a long way down hill before they stopped in the ditch.

It was now Mr. Bliss's turn to laugh; and as he had not laughed since the day before yesterday, with nothing but bother in between, he laughed a lot. He came out and stood in the road, and waved to his friends.

"Good morning!" said the bears, popping their heads over the hedge.

"Lawks!" said Mr. Bliss, jumping into the air.

"Anything we can do for you?" said they.

42

The others fell over one another in their hurry. Fattie and Sergeant Boffin rolled over and over like barrels, quite a long way down hill before they stopped in the ditch.

Twas now Mr. Bliss's turn to laugh; and as he had not laughed since the day before yesterday, with nothing but bother in between, he laughed a lot. He came out and stood in the road, and waved to his friends.

"Good morning!" said the bears, popping their heads over the hedge.

"Lawks!" said Mr. Bliss, jumping into the air.

"Anything we can do for you?" said they.

"No thank you!" said he. "Well — yes, that is not unless you can help me to get my Girabbit out of the house?"

"Certainly!" they said. "Delighted — but not for nothing!"

"Certainly not," said he, "I will remember you."

"You will," said Archie. "I shall send in a bill."

So they came in and shouted up to the Girabbit that they were going to start eating at his tail and work upwards, if he didn't come down and out immediate.

Of course he drew in his neck immediate — in a fine flurry of soot and plaster — but when he looked into the dining-room and saw (he could see very close to) what looked like bears, and what smelt like bears he took such a fright that he jumped bang through the window.

In two more jumps he was over the hedge and in the road.

43

"No thank you!" said he. "Well — yes, that is not unless you can help me to get my girabbit out of the house?"

"Certainly!", they said. "Delighted — but not for nothing!"

"Certainly not", said he; "I will remember you".

"You will", said Archie. "I shall send in a bill.

So they came in, and shouted up to the girabbit that they were going to start eating at his tail and work upwards, if he didn't come down and out immediate.

Of course he drew in his neck immediate — in a fine flurry of soot and plaster —, but when he looked into the dining-room and saw (he could see very close to) what looked like bears, and what smelt like bears he took such a fright that he jumped bang through the window. In two more jumps he was over the hedge and in the road

When the people saw him coming they yelled 'murder!' all together, and ran and rolled faster than before, and every house in the village slammed its doors. As for the Girabbit it never stopped jumping till it was quite lost in the distance; and Mr. Bliss wept big tears at losing it.

After lunch the bears made out a bill for helping; and Mr. Bliss went and got his purse and his money-box, for he thought the time had come to settle up. I thought you would like to see what all these adventures cost him, by the time everything was paid for. It was a _very_ expensive time.

This is a copy of a note Mr. Bliss made in his diary when it was all over.

It quite emptied his money-box (except for one or two foreign coins he kept for collections); so he did not go away for a holiday that summer.

44

When the people saw him coming they yelled 'murder!' all together, and ran and rolled faster than before, and every house in the village slammed its doors.   As for the girabbit it never stopped jumping till it was quite lost in the distance; and Mr. Bliss wept big tears at losing it.

After lunch the bears made out a bill for helping; and Mr. Bliss went and got his purse and his money-box, for he thought the time had come to settle up.   I thought you would like to see what all these adventures cost him, by the time everything was paid for.   It was a very expensive time.

This is a copy of a note Mr. Bliss made in his diary when it was all over.

It quite emptied his money-box (except for one or two foreign coins he kept for collections); so

		£.	s.	d.
Mr Binks	1 motor-car		5.	6.
" "	mending it		3.	0
Mr Day	1 barrow		1.	6.
Mrs Knight	1 cart		3.	6.
Dorkinses	1 soup tureen		.	7
"	hire of ponies		2.	0
Mr Banks (builder & printer)			12.	6
New carpet & rug			7.	6
Tea at Inn (mostly Fatty)			6.	6
Three Bears, for helping			2.	6
Licence for Girabbit			7.	6

carried forward £2. 12. 7

	£.	s.	d.
Brought forward	£.2.	12.	7.
Licence for past			
three years for G.		1.	2. 6
Tip to Sergeant Boffin			6
	£ 3.	15.	7
Add: Damaged hat		.	8½
Damage to clothes			4
Total.	£ 3.	16.	7½

— June 14th. T. Bliss.

he did not go away for a holiday that Summer.

That afternoon, as soon as he had said goodbye to the bears, he took all his money, got on his bicycle, and went down to the village. He paid Mr. Binks and Mr. Day and Mrs. Knight on the spot (and sent postal orders to the Dorkinses and the Innkeeper). They said they knew he was a gentleman all the time.

As a matter of fact Mr. Bliss never used the motor-car again — he had taken a great dislike to it. So he gave it to Mr. Day as a wedding-present. Yes, wedding-present. Very soon after this Mr. Day became Mrs. Knight's third husband. She said it seemed suitable, seeing how they were both in the same line of business, and had had a lot of adventures together. So they set up a green-grocers shop in the village, and called it "Day and Knight's."

45

That afternoon, as soon as he had said goodbye to the bears, he took all his money, got on his bicycle, and went down to the village. He paid Mr. Binks and Mr. Day and Mrs. Knight on the spot (and sent postal orders to the Dorkinses (and the Innkeeper). They said they knew he was a gentleman all the time.

As a matter of fact Mr. Bliss never used the motor-car again — he had taken a great dislike to it. So he gave it to Mr. Day as a wedding-present. Yes, wedding-present. Very soon after this Mr. Day became Mrs. Knight's third husband. She said it seemed suitable, seeing how they were both in the same line of business, and had a lot of adventures together. So they set up a green-grocers shop in the village, and called it "Day and Knight's".

They are very friendly with Mr. Bliss now, and they always let him have bananas and cabbages very cheap.

There were great doings at the wedding. Mr. Bliss played his concertina. Fattie Dorkins sang a comic song, but as it was all about policemen with large feet, Sergeant Boffin did not laugh. The bears drank everybody's health several times, and did not go home till next morning. But best of all, in the middle of it the Girabbit put his head in through the window!

"Ha! Ha!" he said. "Here we all are again."

And everybody choked.

46

They are very friendly with Mr Bliss now, and they always let him have bananas and cabbages very cheap.

There were great doings at the wedding. Mr Bliss played his concertina. Fattie Dorkins sang a comic song, but as it was all about policemen with large feet, Sergeant Boffin did not laugh. The bears drank every-body's health several times, and did not go home till next morning. But best of all, in the middle of it the girabbit put his head in through the window!

"Ha! ha!" he said. "Here
we all are again".
And everybody choked

"Where <u>have</u> you been?" said Mr. Bliss.

"Ha! ha!" said he, "wouldn't you like to know! Ask the Dorkinses and the bears!"

That's why the Dorkinses left early. They did not like the sound of it. But just then the bears did not care what happened, though they changed their minds when they <u>did</u> get home.

The Girabbit had eaten every bit of food in their house, and broken the pantry window.

As for the Dorkinses, they found he had bitten the tops off every tree in their orchard, and made an enormous hole in the night right in the middle of their best lawn.

The bears said: "Well we're blowed! Old Bliss has got the best of it after all", and they left it at that. But the Dorkinses sent in a bill again, and while they were about it they added on a charge for the bears' cabbages, which they had forgotten about: total £1. 9. 8.

But Mr. Bliss had got no money at the moment, and he was getting rather tired of the Dorkinses, so sent them fourpence in stamps, and a bill of his own.

This is how he made it out.

When the Dorkinses got this they were very annoyed, and Mr. B. and they have not been particularly friendly since.

47

"Where <u>have</u> you been?" said Mr. Bliss

"Ha! ha!" said he, "wouldn't you like to know!" Ask the Dorkinses and the bears!"

That's why the Dorkinses left early. They did not like the sound of it. But just then the bears did not care what happened, though they changed their minds when they <u>did</u> get home. The girabbit had eaten every bit of food in their house, and broken the pantry window.

As for the Dorkinses, they found he had bitten the tops off every tree in their orchard, and made an enormous hole in the night, right in the middle of their best lawn.

The bears said: "Well we're blowed! Old Bliss has got the best of it after all", and they left it at that. But the Dorkinses sent in a bill again, and while they were about it they added on a charge for the bears' cabbages, which they had forgotten about: total £ 1 .. 9 .. 8. But Mr. Bliss had got no money at the moment, and he was getting rather tired of the Dorkinses, so sent them fourpence in stamps, and a bill of his own.

This is how he made it out.

When the Dorkins got this they were very annoyed, and Mr. B. and they have not been particularly friendly since.

Dorkins Bros.
Dr. to J. Bliss

To trampling on my flowerbeds @ 10d. each	3 . 4d .
To J. Dawkins tea at Inn	6 .. 0d
To frightening valuable Girabbit	£1/0 . 0
	£1/9/4
Balance in stamps	4
	1 . 9 . 8

Yrs sincerely J. Bliss.

But Mr. Bliss is quite happy, though the village children are always trespassing in his garden, to catch a glimpse of the Girabbit. He drives a little donkey cart now, not a motor, and Sergeant Boffin salutes him every time he appears in the village.

"'Ow's yer little pet, sir?'' says he.

"Nicely, thank you,'' says Mr. B., "but hard on cabbages. And how are all the Boffinses?''

"Nicely, thank you,'' says he, "but cruel hard on shoe-leather.''

And that is the end of the story — except that Mr. Bliss threw the green hat away (and the Girabbit found it on the dustheap), and he wears a white hat now in summer, and a brown in winter. And that is all.

There is just one more picture, over the page.

48

But Mr. Bliss is quite happy, though the village children are always trespassing in his garden, to catch a glimpse of the Girabbit. He drives a little donkey cart now, not a motor, and Sergeant Boffin salutes him every time he appears in the village

"Ow's yer little pet, sir?" says he.

"Nicely thank you," says Mr. B., "but hard on cabbages". And how are all the Boffinses?"

"Nicely thank you", says he, "but cruel hard on shoe-leather".

And that's the end of the story — except that Mr. Bliss threw the green hat away (and the Girabbit found it on the dustheap), and he wears a white hat now in summer, and a brown in winter. And that is all.

There is just one more picture, over the page.

The End.

The End.

NOTE

Before *The Hobbit* had been published, Professor Tolkien wrote and illustrated *Mr. Bliss* to amuse his own children — as well, evidently, as himself. Now, after more than fifty years, it has been made available to the general public for the first time. This facsimile edition reproduces the charming pencil and watercolor illustrations and the hand-lettered text.

Tolkien himself had bought a motorcar in 1932 and suffered some misadventures that prompted him to produce this book, which his biographer Humphrey Carpenter describes as being a little like Edward Lear and a little like Beatrix Potter.

It is quite unlike anything else Tolkien has done and has a puckish charm for children and grownups alike.

NOTE

Before *The Hobbit* had been published, Professor Tolkien wrote and illustrated *Mr. Bliss* to amuse his own children — as well, evidently, as himself. Now, after more than fifty years, it has been made available to the general public for the first time. This facsimile edition reproduces the charming pencil and watercolor illustrations and the hand-lettered text.

Tolkien himself had bought a motorcar in 1932 and suffered some misadventures that prompted him to produce this book, which his biographer Humphrey Carpenter describes as being a little like Edward Lear and a little like Beatrix Potter.

It is quite unlike anything else Tolkien has done and has a puckish charm for children and grownups alike.